A PAIR OF RED SNEAKERS

A PAIR OF RED SNEAKERS

Lisa Lawston

Pictures by **BB Sams**

Orchard Books • New York

To Zoē and Izabelle
—L.L.

To Barbara
—BB Sams

Text copyright © 1998 by Lisa Lawston
Illustrations copyright © 1998 by BB Sams

Orchard Books, 95 Madison Avenue, New York, NY 10016

Manufactured in the United States of America. Printed by Barton Press, Inc.
Bound by Horowitz/Rae. Book design by Mina Greenstein and Anahid Hamparian

The text of this book is set in 16 point Stone Sans.
The illustrations are grease pencil and art markers.
2 4 6 8 10 9 7 5 3 1

Library of Congress Cataloging-in-Publication Data
Lawston, Lisa. A pair of red sneakers / by Lisa Lawston ; illustrated by BB Sams.   p.   cm.
Summary: At the sneaker store, Miles asks for a stunning, stupendous, sensational sneaker, with outrageous and notable features like attachable toes, suction-cup grips, and inflatable floats.
ISBN 0-531-30104-4 (trade : alk. paper). — ISBN 0-531-33104-0 (lib. bdg. : alk. paper)   [1. Shoes—Fiction. 2. Stories in rhyme.]   I. Sams, BB, ill.   II. Title.   PZ8.3.L39Pai   1998   [E]—dc21   98-10481

"May I help you?" the man in the sneaker store said.
"Yes," replied Miles. "I know what I want, and I want them in red."

"The sneaker with long attachable toes for building tree houses with views of rainbows."

"For swinging off branches to neighboring trees, where they'll offer me donuts and crackers and cheese."

"The sneaker with circular suction-cup grips for windy-day sailing on slippery ships."

"With inflatable floats, propelled by small motors, and a compass for saving lost fish and stray boaters."

"The sneaker with bouncers for jumping and soaring . . .

. . . with oversized pouncers for safely exploring basketball hoops,
rooftops and stars, the Statue of Liberty, and life on Mars."

"The sneaker that has four adjustable wheels for rolling and gliding through parks and through fields.

"The self-balancing kind that prevent nasty spills 'round the sharpest of curves, down the steepest of hills."

"The sneaker with star-studded parachute ties for diving or gliding through sunshiny skies."

"With umbrella pop-ups in case it should rain, and fast-flapping wings to fly back to the plane, so that you can dive off again and again."

"The sneaker, the shoe, with the tough attitude for when bullying bullies is what you must do. With shark jaws it retrieves your lunch from your foe, then chomps on his backpack and stomps on his toe."

"The sneaker that's said to be truly amazing if the Amazon jungle is where you're trailblazing."

"With tarantula whistles, mosquito confusers . . .

. . . jaguar reflectors, and boa amusers."

"The sneaker with rubber-eraser tips, for rubbing out traffic on long family trips—

for rubbing out spinach or meat on your plate, and erasing those messes that Mom and Dad hate."

"The sneaker, the pair with the bubblegum blocks, for scaling
and clinging to treacherous rocks, for exploring Spike Mountain and
Percible's Peak, with enough gum left over to chew for a week."

"The sneaker, the pair it's a comfort to wear when visiting doctors, or the dentist's big chair. They quietly soothe, adhered to your feet, and hug toes and soles till your visit's complete."

"The sneaker designed for prancing, enhancing...rapping, tapping, jazzing, and dancing."

"The ballet sneaker for showing your guests the springiest, wingiest, best pirouettes."

"The sneaker, the one with the mega-speed pack, for racing and running and staying on track. Programmed to win, they press on till you've won . . .

". . . then ten little fans cool your toes when you're done."

"That is the sneaker I want, please," Miles said. "I want that sneaker, and I want it in red."

The man in the sneaker store answered
directly, "The sneaker you want,
if I heard you correctly, is that stunning,
stupendous, sensational sneaker,
the one with outrageous and notable
features like: attachable toes,
suction-cup grips, inflatable floats,
rubberized tips ...
bouncers, pouncers,
adjustable wheels,
fans for your toes—
but not for your heels—
umbrella pop-ups,
parachute ties,
fast-flapping wings
in case you should fly,
the danciest sneaker,
a comfort to wear,
with bubblegum blocks and
bubbles to spare ...
the sneaker with attitude,
it's great for trailblazing
the light, compact sneaker
that's truly amazing."

"The sneaker that offers the largest collection
of plentiful patterns and color selections like:
tidal-wave turquoise, angel-wing white,
orange daredevil, fuchsia le fright ...
purple perfection, leopardy spots, three shades of paisley,
pink polka dots...crackling yellow,
cloud-climbing blue, swinging sienna,
black bubbly too...four perky plaids,
fresh Martian green, and
all of the patterns and
shades in between.

"However," the man in the
sneaker store said,
"we're completely sold out
of that sneaker in red."

"Sold out!" Miles said with a shake of his head, as he stared at the pile of rubber and thread. "What good is a sneaker if it isn't in red?"

And he went on to buy blue sandals instead.